To Lily

Best Wishes

Jim Moore

11/05/04

the ALL ANIMAL BAND

Written by Jim Moore
Illustrated by Norris Hall

Productions, Inc.
Mt. Juliet, TN
www.theanimalband.com

Library of Congress Control Number: 2004092378

ISBN 0-9752619-0-8

Printed in Hong Kong   First Edition

10 9 8 7 6 5 4 3 2 1

Published by

Productions, Inc.
P.O. Box 392
Mt. Juliet, Tennessee 37121

Website: www.theanimalband.com

Look for these exciting music CDs and Videos:
"Animal Rock" - CD
"Are We There Yet?" - CD
"Imagination Dance" - CD
"Imagination Dance" - DVD/VHS
"Uncaged" - CD

Willie the Squirrel's bushy tail swished from side to side. Musicians played at the park ranger's house, and Willie swayed and tapped to the beat of every song. When the people stopped playing and went inside, Willie jumped to the ground.

He scampered up to the guitar and sniffed it.
Then he touched the polished wood and slid his paws
along the strings. It made an awful screeching sound.

It wasn't anything like the beautiful music he had heard.

The squirrel climbed onto the upright bass, but one of his sharp claws got tangled in a string. When he yanked it loose, the big bass made a kind of rumble that reminded Willie of the noise his tummy made when it was hungry.

He jumped onto the drummer's seat. He took a cautious look around. Then he picked up a stick and lightly touched the round metal cymbal. *Tiiiinnnggg!*

He turned to the snare drum and whacked it. The noise scared him so badly, he knocked over the drum and it fell into the cymbal with a loud crash! Willie cleared the fence in one jump as the musicians ran out of the house.

That night Willie's dreams were filled with lovely music.
More than anything he wanted to be a musician and make wonderful music, too!

The next morning, Willie headed straight for Ollie the Owl's roosting limb. Ollie was sound asleep, but Willie was too excited to care.

"Ollie! Ollie! Wake up!" shouted Willie.

Ollie blinked and nearly fell off the limb.

"For the love of nature, kid. What is it now?" Ollie grumbled.

Willie always seemed to have a new scheme up his sleeve, and he always just had to tell Ollie in the morning.

"How would you like to be in an all-animal band?" said Willie.

Ollie scowled and said, "Squirrel, you're plucking my feathers! Whoooo ever heard of such a thing? You've been eating out of too many of those bird feeders at the ranger's cabin!"

Ollie nodded off to sleep again and Willie quietly backed down the tree.

t the bottom of the tree he found his friends Fredi the Frog, Dan the Dog, and Slick the Snake on eir way to the lake for a swim. Willie excitedly told them about his latest idea: animal musicians!

"Gosh, I don't know about that," said Dan.

"Just come with me tonight. You'll see," said Willie.

That night Willie and Ollie hid in the big oak tr

"This had better be good, kid," said Ollie.

"You are such a gentleman," said Fredi
as Slick helped her to a seat.

Dan's nose was busy inspecting all of
the wonderful smells by the fence.

Suddenly, the cabin door opened and laughter spilled out onto the lawn.

"Here they come!" barked Dan.

The people tuned their instruments. Then the drummer counted and the lively music began.

Willie pretended to play guitar. Ollie couldn't keep his head still, and Slick did a charming snake dance.

Fredi began to croak and Dan put his paws over his mouth to keep from howling.

Finally one of the musicians shouted, "It's time for a break!" And they went inside.

"Do we dare?" whispered Slick.

"Whoooo's stopping us?" said Ollie as he glided down and landed next to the upright bass. He flipped a string with his wing and the deep *hummmm* tickled him. He thumped it.

He grinned and danced a jig.

While Dan watched out for the humans, Fredi hopped up to the crackling fire and began her evening vocal warm-up. "Jeremiah was a bullfrog, la, la, la, la, la, la," she sang.

Slick slithered over to the drum and couldn't resist striking the big bass drum. But when his nose hit the tight drum, it bounced him backwards! *B-o-i-n-g!*

"Cool!" he said.

Willie jumped from the tree and almost crashed into the guitar, he was so excited.

He ran his paw down the neck of the instrument. This time the strings quivered and twanged, but they didn't screech.

Maybe he *could* make music!

Suddenly Dan woofed the alarm, "They're coming back!"

The animals scrambled under the fence, but they couldn't help looking back at the beautiful shiny instruments. They looked at each other, and then and there they decided: they would form the world's only all-animal band!

The
wee

"We
said

The next day, the band went to work.

Slick searched for hollow logs to make into drums.

Ollie and Willie gave Bucky Beaver designs for making the bass and guitar.

Bucky used his sharp teeth to gnaw tree limbs into wonderful shapes. Then he used his rough tail to polish the wood until it shone.

At last, they were ready for their first show. Creatures came from all over the woods to hear the band.

Slick counted, "One, two, three, four," and the band began to play.

Ollie plucked the bass. Slick beat the drums. Willie strummed the guitar. Dan's and Fredi's voices blended together in perfect harmony. They sounded great!

A giant cheer rose up from the forest.

The next day, the band went to work.

Slick searched for hollow logs to make into drums.

Ollie and Willie gave Bucky Beaver designs for making the bass and guitar.

Bucky used his sharp teeth to gnaw tree limbs into wonderful shapes. Then he used his rough tail to polish the wood until it shone.

The strings were woven by ten thousand spiders and were guaranteed not to break.

They practiced for days and
weeks and months.

"We're going to be the best ever!"
said Willie.

At last, they were ready for their first show. Creatures came from all over the woods to hear the band.

Slick counted, "One, two, three, four," and the band began to play.

Ollie plucked the bass. Slick beat the drums. Willie strummed the guitar. Dan's and Fredi's voices blended together in perfect harmony. They sounded great!

A giant cheer rose up from the forest.

The animals didn't know it, but someone else was listening, too.

Just as the band finished a rousing encore, a tall man stepped out from behind the trees, clapping and smiling.

"A human!" cried a raccoon.

All of the animals gasped and scattered into the woods.

Willie scrambled for a nearby tree.
"Please don't go," cried the man. "I want to share
your talent with the world."

"Talent?" thought Willie.
He swallowed, stopped, and
turned around to face
the man.

He was one of the musicians
from the ranger's cabin!

"My name is Elroy J. Gigaway, of Gigaway Talent Agency, and I can make you big stars."

"Big stars?" thought Willie.
The squirrel hopped a little closer.

"Your music is wonderful!"

"Really?" asked Willie.

The man nodded and smiled. "You're real musicians."

Musicians! Real musicians. Willie glanced up at the rest of the band, who watched from their hiding places.

Then Willie smiled, too. A big smile!

And Willie and Mr. Gigaway shook hand to paw. It was a deal.
Elroy J. Gigaway was going to make them famous!

he next morning all of the band members gathered around while Elroy told them stories of faraway
aces and musical adventures. He told them about famous bands such as the Beatles, the Byrds,
e Turtles, and even a group called Hootie and the Blowfish.

llie wondered if Hootie was a distant relative.

hen Elroy told the band to go pack their instruments.
hey were off on a grand world tour!

All of the woodland folk gathered to see them off. They howled, growled, snorted, and squeale their support as a shiny red truck drove away.

"Good-bye!" shouted Ollie and Dan and Fredi and Slick.

"Thanks, everybody!" cried Willie. "Good-bye!"

Willie was sure they would be back someday, but for now he couldn't wait to show people all over the world the first ever, the one and only all-animal band!

This book is based on the song:

ALL ANIMAL BAND

This is a story about Fredi the Frog
And a puppy dog named Dan
They loved to sing and play so much
They formed an all–animal band
Willie the Squirrel plays lead guitar
And Ollie the Owl plays bass
Slick the Snake doesn't have any hands
So he beats the drums with his face

Fredi the Frog and Dan the Dog
Can sing any song on the list
When the animal band gets together to play
It sounds a little something like this

A bark and a ribbit and a diddley do
A whoo, a chuckle and a hiss
Twang and a thump
Rump-a-dump dump
Not a single note do they miss

One day a man came along
And heard the all–animal band
He said, "I can make you all big stars
You can travel all over the land
So they all loaded up in a big ole truck
And left with their hopes and dreams
They played for the Pope and the President
Who loved to hear them sing

A bark and a ribbit and a diddley do
A whoo, a chuckle and a hiss
Twang and a thump
And a rump-a-dump dump
Not a single note do they miss

Jim Moore
© 1989 Animal Band Music (ASCAP)

As recorded on the CD "Are We There Yet?" (1992)
by The Animal Band